FARM FRIENDS CLEAN UP

BY Cristina Garelli

ILLUSTRATED BY Francesca Chessa

Crown Publishers 👑 New York

To Julia, Sara, and Sabina —C.G.

For everybody who loves me, in spite of all —F.C.

Library of Congress Cataloging-in-Publication Data
Garelli, Cristina
Farm friends clean up / by Cristina Garelli ; illustrated by Francesca Chessa.—1st ed.
p.   cm.
Summary: Frolicking farm animals learn about good hygiene.
[1. Cleanliness—Fiction. 2. Health—Fiction. 3. Domestic animals—Fiction.] I. Chessa, Francesca, ill.
II. Title.
PZ7. G17937Far   2000

ISBN 0-517-80081-0 (trade)
0-517-80082-9 (lib. bdg.)

10 9 8 7 6 5 4 3 2 1
October 2000
First Edition

BRUSH YOUR TEETH, WOLF!

CUT YOUR HAIR, SHEEP!

TAKE A BATH, PIG!

BRUSH YOUR TEETH, WOLF!

This is Wolf.

His favorite game is chasing his
farm friends and scaring them
with his big teeth!

But Dog is not running away.

"Aren't you afraid of me?" asks Wolf.

"No, I'm not. You have such dirty teeth."

"Look at <u>my</u> smile," says Dog.
"What can I do to look like you?"
asks Wolf.

"You have to brush your teeth up and down every day," Wolf's farm friends agree. "Here is a toothbrush and toothpaste!"

"Look at me now!" says Wolf,
proud of his perfect smile.

"Now you're really scary!

We can play together again.

Catch us if you can!"

CUT YOUR HAIR, SHEEP!

Sheep was always the best
at catching the ball, until...

"What happened to you, Sheep?"
ask her farm friends.
"First, I tripped over my hair.

Then I couldn't
see the ball,

and now I'm stuck in the gate," answers Sheep. "And all because of my hair. What a day!"

"How would you like me to cut your hair?" asks Cat.

"I don't know. Just try not to cut it too short!" answers Sheep.

"Well, Sheep, what do you think?" asks Cat.

"Oh, my. I will <u>never</u> go out looking like this!"

Sheep answers.

"Come outside, Sheep!" say her farm friends.

"Everybody is going to like your haircut.

And we want to play ball!"

"You look great!"
Goat says. "Now it's my
turn to have my hair cut!"

"I'll make you look fantastic."

TAKE A BATH, PIG!

Pig is truly a pig. His farm friends are sure that he has never taken a bath.

Pig's favorite game is hide-and-go-seek.

He loves to hide in piles of dirt!

"What a mess!" says Dog. "I'll look for Pig somewhere else. I don't want to get dirty!"

"What's that smell?" says Cow. "It reminds me of our dirty laundry basket! We'd better go help find Pig. It's getting late!"

"It's dark out and we're tired of looking for Pig," say the farm friends. "Let's go home!"

"Why did you leave me hiding in that pile of dirt?" asks Pig.

"We didn't know you were there," his friends answer. "You are so dirty that you blended right in!"

"Well, taking a bath is not so bad after all!"